TESS
THE TRACTOR

Peter Bently • Sébastien Chebret

Quarto
Library

One morning, the vehicles arrived at Whizzy Wheels Academy to find their teacher, Rusty the pickup truck, had sprayed water on the school track.

"Good morning, class," he said. "Today you're going to learn how to drive safely on wet roads."

"Huh, that's *easy*," said Tess the tractor. "All you need are big wheels like mine."

One by one, the vehicles set off along the track.

"Stay well back from the vehicle in front," said Rusty.
"And drive slowly and steadily to avoid skidding."

"This is too slow for me," said Tess.
"Anyway, tractors don't skid!"

She sped up and overtook the other vehicles.

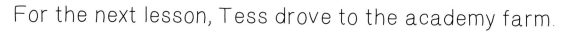

For the next lesson, Tess drove to the academy farm.

"First, some simple off-road skills," said Rusty.
"You can start by driving across the field."

Tess was asked to drive to the
top of a steep hill...

...and down again.

"Still too easy!" she said.

Then Tess got to practice pulling different trailers.

"See if you can pull the plow in a straight line," said Rusty.

Tess went a bit wobbly at first, but she soon got the hang of it.

"We tractors are great at steering!" said Tess.

Next, Tess learned how to cut hay. She got her lines perfectly straight the first time.

Finally, Tess practiced pulling a baler
over the grass. It scooped up the grass
and turned it into neat bales of hay.

"Nice work!" said Rusty. "After our break,
you can take the bales to the barn."

But during the break, it suddenly started to rain. When Tess and Rusty returned, the fields were very muddy.

Tess drove up and down while Lenny the loader tractor lifted the bales onto her trailer.

"Can't we go any *faster*?" moaned Tess.

"You have to be careful in
this mud," said Rusty.

"Now let's get the bales into the barn before it rains again," said Rusty.

"I'm going to take a short cut," said Tess.
She revved her engine and set off through the mud.

"Wait, there are cows in the next field!" warned Rusty.

But Tess didn't listen as she sped off. "Tractors can do *anything*!" she boasted.

Tess went faster
and faster.

"It *is* a bit muddy," she thought. "But my
big tires and powerful engine can manage!"

Tess bounced and bumped across
the field. She suddenly saw a
cow right in front of her!

"Yikes!" she cried.

Tess slammed on her brakes, but she
couldn't stop in the deep, slippery mud.

Tess swerved and toppled over
with a great big

SPLOSH!

Rusty and Lenny helped pull Tess upright.
She was very muddy but otherwise okay.

"I tried to warn you about
the cows," said Rusty.

"I'm sorry I didn't listen," said Tess.

"A tractor can do lots of things, but from now on I'll be a lot more careful."

Let's look at
TESS

Trailer

Tow bar

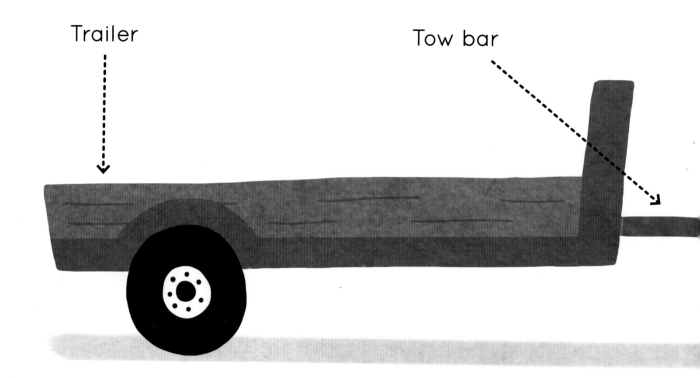